Round Up at The Burger Bar
Parts 1-5
The Beginning

Russ Crossley

3RD STREET — PUBLISHING

Round Up at The Burger Bar
Parts 1-5
The Beginning
Russ Crossley

ISBN 978-1-927621-32-5

This is a work of fiction. The persons and situations
are products of the authors imagination,

Published by 53rd Street Publishing
www.53rdstreetpublising.com

Authors note

This book collects the first five parts of
the serial novel Round Up At The Burger bar: The
Legend of Trixie Pug. By the year 3333 1/3 massive
fast food corporations control the galaxy. Trixie will
become the galaxy's 2nd most powerful CEO for a
fast food franchise called Heavenly Sky Burger. To
read more about Trixie check out the short story, *Big
Business* and the novel *Attack of the Lushites*.

These stories reveal the early adventures of
Trixie and her friend Cherry Bomb thirty years before
she becomes a CEO. In these stories you will discover
how Trixie became the hungry woman she eventually
becomes.

The story is satire and meant to be a funny,
satirical take on a possible future, and like any good
SF answers the question what if fast food corporations
controlled the galaxy and the future? What problems
would occur, and how would we overcome them?

I truly hope you read this story in the light
it was meant and enjoy the ride and laugh at the
absurdities that occur sometimes when you ask these
questions.

Russ Crossley
March 2012

Dedication

For Rita, for everything. Thanks, honey, for your love and support.

About the Author

International selling author, Russ Crossley writes science fiction and fantasy, and mystery/suspense under the name R.G. Crossley.

His latest science fiction satire set in the far future, *Revenge of the Lushites*, is a sequel to *Attack of the Lushites* released in 2011. The latest title in the series was released in the fall of 2013. Both titles are available in e-book and trade paperback.

He has sold several short stories that have appeared in anthologies from various publishers including; WMG Publishing, Pocket Books, and St. Martins Press.

He is a member of SF Canada and is past president of the Greater Vancouver Chapter of Romance Writers of America. He is also an alumni of the Oregon Coast Professional Fiction Writers Master Class taught by award winning author/editors, Kristine Katherine Rusch and Dean Wesley Smith.

Feel free to contact him on Facebook, Twitter, or his website http:www.russcrossley.com. He loves to hear from readers

Acknowledgements

Many thanks to my editor, Cindie Geddes, at Lucky Bat Books, who's also a fan of this universe, for her work on this project. Together we're building a wonderful and funny new myth for the 21st century and beyond.

Table of Contents

Part 1

Eating anything deep fried is better than not eating at all.

— Deep-Fry McChuckle, Official Mascot of Heavenly Sky Burger, speaking at the grand opening of outlet number 3,343,0001

TRIXIE AIOLI PUSHED THE MOP ONCE across the gray tiled floor and stopped. Sweat poured off her shiny forehead into her eyes stinging them something terrible. She blinked repeatedly as she collapsed into her hover chair.

She sighed with relief as the automated body contour function enveloped her tired, ponderous frame. One more swipe of the floor and she knew she'd die of exhaustion.

Part 1

So far she'd only pushed the mop once, but once was more than a normal human being could handle. It begged the question, "Why do we have robots and aliens?" To do the manual labor of course!

Why did Mr. Pickles-On-The-Side have to pick on her all the time? She wasn't the one who swapped out the condiment bar with pizza toppings, and it wasn't her who filled the dumpster, out back of the Heavenly Sky Burger outlet, with used pizza take-out boxes.

She'd long suspected Kelp Shaker was behind these pranks, and sensed he was setting her up to take a fall. The guy was a real butt kisser who'd made it clear he hated Trixie. If she didn't fight back soon she'd lose this job, and with it any chance of taking control of this burger empire.

Ever since she'd graduated from Burger University with a degree in Restaurant Domination and Market Saturation (with a minor in Employee Subjugation) she'd been planning to out-scratch, out-claw, out-crawl, and out-eat her way up the corporate ranks until she had gathered her forces to launch a totally hostile take over. No small order fries like Pickles-On-The-Side or Kelp Shaker were going to stand in her way.

Kelp had to go, along with his grease-stained shadow.

And I'm just the woman to take him down.

Her breathing came in ragged gasps, and her heart beat hard in her chest. *That is if I don't die of a heart attack first.* She pulled a disposable handkerchief out of her one-size-fits-all-no-matter-how-big-you-are baby-blue jumpsuit pocket with her sausage -sized digits (something she was very proud of) and used it to wipe her forehead of streams of sweat.

It was a good thing the chair had a built-in Heart Attack Safety System (patent pending since 2895.6). Trixie was certain with HASS installed she'd live to a ripe old age of two hundred and fifty just like everyone else. Provided she didn't have to mop the floor too often.

Mr. Pickles-On-The-Side appeared in his hover chair from around the wall that separated the storeroom from the hallway. His office was located midway down the hall separating the trash launch disposal system at the back of the restaurant from the kitchen at the other end. Garbage in, garbage out, and rocketed into space. The circle of fast food life.

Pickles-On-The-Side, a hugely handsome man that spilled over the arms of his hover chair with black greasy hair and little black pig-like eyes, was glaring at her. "Done yet?" he said in his reedy voice.

Part 1

Pickles-On-The-Side had been manager at this outlet for fifty-two years.

She dropped the soaking handkerchief into a disposal can where it was vaporized. She had no idea how the can worked, only that the handkerchief disappeared. A good thing. It had often occurred to her someone should invent a larger disposal can and save the trouble of launching the trash into space. Not my job. "Yes, sir, I made the daily swipe with the mop just as you instructed, sir."

Pickles-On-The-Side's heavy jowls relaxed and his beady eyes, as black as onyx, softened. Trixie had always thought of him as such a handsome man, though he was too old for her, and he was married to a burger cook in store number 47,000A.

If only I could be so fortunate as to marry a burger cook I'd be literally swimming in burgers. Her mouth watered at the thought.

He floated to within a few feet of her before he spoke again.

"Good job, Aioli. You may make a good deep-fry cook yet." His chair swiveled in midair until his back was to her. "Hushpuppy!" he called. "Finish mopping the storeroom." With that he floated away and quickly disappeared around the wall once again.

4

With a soft puff of air, Hushpuppy came around the corner from the opposite direction of the hallway that Pickles-On-The-Side had disappeared down. He was a janitor-bot, with a round silver body, long arms with fully articulated hands and fingers, and a head made of clear glass with two cameras where the eyes would be on a human that could swivel ninety degrees to each side. Like her hover chair he rode on antigravity waves. The one design flaw that had always bothered Trixie was the designer hadn't given him a nose, mouth, or eyebrows. Hushpuppy had no face.

"Hi, Trixie, how's it cookin'?" said the bot, in his usual friendly manner. Even if he had no face Trixie had grown fond of him.

Trixie's brow wrinkled. "Not exactly the way I planned my career would be cookin' by now, if you know what I mean."

Hushpuppy floated over to the mop where Trixie had leaned it against the wall, wrapped his articulated fingers around the handle, and began to mop the floor furiously. Covering the remainder of the floor in seconds. "I know what you mean," said Hushpuppy in an earnest tone of voice.

Trixie chuckled. "Oh, Hushpuppy, you say the sweetest things. If I didn't know you were a bot I'd think you had a crush on me."

Part 1

She floated away intending to check the trash launch disposal system to see if it was full enough for another launch.

One of her jobs was to make sure the trash didn't build up too much. One hundred years after the Fast Food Only Act was passed in the year 2349, when the great-great-great grandson of the famous Atlanta Fried Kicken Company was President of the World States, trash disposal became a major problem as sales increased exponentially across Dirt.

Finally, in the year 2450 a Garbageologitst named Compactor, devised a new invention whereby he created Big Balls of Garbage. The idea was to stuff garbage in planet-sized gravity nets that held the trash tightly together then shoot them into space into decaying orbits around the sun. The plan was that the Big Balls would burn up in the sun heat. Simple. Problem solved. What could go wrong? Of course once the Big Balls were launched, no one bothered to check if they were actually destroyed by the sun, but then why would they? It was logical, and logic didn't need checking.

Before she disappeared around the corner she added, "Hushpuppy, my career is stalled until I can do something about Kelp. He hates me. And he sucks up to Mr. Pickles-On-The-Side."

Trixie sighed to herself. She'd slept during the lectures on sucking up to the boss given by Professor Pump Aggravation because she believed hard work with a dash of laziness would always prevail over butt kissing. It had worked for her father, he'd been head waiter at Nacho Taco for over sixty years, and was the laziest hard worker she'd ever known.

When she arrived at the trash launch bay, which was piled high enough that the trash almost touched the twenty-foot high ceiling with gray garbage bags, she was startled as Hushpuppy appeared from behind her. The bot seemed agitated, as evidenced by his camera eyes flitting back and forth in quick fleeting movements.

"What is it, pal?" she asked. "You wanta help me load trash into the next rocket launcher?" Oh, brother, she thought, he's not a dog for goodness sake. He's my friend, who just happens to be a janitor-bot.

"Huh, sorry about that, HP."

"For what?"

Trixie's cheeks grew warm. "Never mind."

"Anyway, Trixie, I may have a solution for your problem with Kelp, and it may advance your career."

That last part really got her attention.

Kelp was gonna get his in the end when she shoved a burger flipper up his rear—when she made head burger cook in three years. (Her promotion schedule was pretty well laid out in her own mind; flunky, assistant to the assistant janitor, head janitor, assistant to the assistant deep fry cook (a yummy job since she would then be a test taster for new products), assistant deep fry cook, deep fry cook, assistant to the assistant burger cook, assistant burger cook, head burger cook—and that was only the beginning of her climb to fame and fortune).

In ten years she'd have Mr. Pickles-On-The-Side's job, and then she would begin to gather her allies for the hostile takeover she had planned. In thirty years she'd not only love the products (burgers ruled, pizza sucked) the company would be in her greasy grip.

I am a genius.

"Ok, HP, tell me."

The bot swiveled his head from one side to the other side, then his camera eyes steadied on her. It was like he was afraid someone would be listening (which they probably were given the fast food business was a cheese grinder.) "I have a friend at Janitor University who has a friend who knows someone." The bot paused then added, "Someone you will want to meet."

"Who?" Trixie said anxiously barely able to contain her excitement. Her heart rate increased, so her chair injected her with a sedative to stabilize her heart pace. Within milliseconds her heart rate slowed and a feeling of euphoria came over her.

I have a good feeling about this.

"Zippy Piner," said HP, his tone laced with pride.

Trixie blinked. "Who or what is a Zippy Piner?"

"She's invented a new type of starship she calls a Marketeer."

A Marketeer? The Intergalactic League of Fast Food Giants already had all the known star ship existing, designs copyrighted, registered, protected, and monopolized. No one dared attempt to compete with them, or their plethora of lawyers would crush them under their big fat thumbs. Not a bad way to go, but Trixie lay down for crushing under anyone's big fat thumbs.

What had this Zippy Piner done that could break the back of that monopoly, that wouldn't end with her being the assistant to the assistant bottle washer at a low-level fast food franchise outlet on one of the outer rim worlds?

Trixie shuddered at the thought of the kind of life for those working on the outer rim.

Part 1

Supply lines were stretched crispy fry thin, and were often interrupted by food pirates. Consequently most workers on the rim worlds were thinner than their inner worlds counterparts, and only ate four meals a day. Even thinking about missing two meals a day made Trixie queasy. The horror. The horror.

If this Zippy had invented a new type of starship that could break the backs of the League then she would be the up-and-comer she had been hoping to meet. Trixie hesitated. Wait. Why would Zippy help her? She didn't need a once-a-day floor swiper.

"I'm confused, HP, why would this Zippy person who invented a starship need me?"

"For access to your boyfriend, of course."

Trixie's wide sweaty forehead wrinkled. Boyfriend? Her features abruptly softened when she realized who the bot was talking about. She'd told HP about her schoolgirl crush on a certain rocket scientist she'd dated a few times. But Herman Pug? The skinny rocket scientist from her Marketing to Dominate the Competition class at the university?

Sure, she liked Herman, he was smart and charming, but he was also wayyyy too skinny.

The guy probably weighted no more than two hundred pounds, and he'd confessed to her one night over dinner he'd even lost three pounds while studying for the final exam. Imagine losing weight doing school work?

As her digestive consultant used to say, a meal break every hour is essential in maintaining good health. Trixie kept to a strict regime of eating between classes and maintained hourly eating breaks during long hours of study.

Proudly she gained weight every semester, in fact she hoped one day to win the coveted "She Who Dies the Fattest Wins" Award at the end of her life. She sighed. If you don't dream big what would be the point of living?

Trixie chuckled, causing her belly to jiggle and her heavy jowls to flap. "I hope you don't mean Herman Pug. I haven't talked to him in a year. Besides he's probably involved with someone else by now."

"So you think he's interesting then?" said HP. Trixie would later swear he had wiggled his eyebrows in a suggestive manner, if he had eyebrows, which he didn't.

"OK. I admit, Herman's interesting, but not interested, if you know what I mean."

"Oh, I wouldn't be so sure about that if I were you."

Trixie eyed the robot. Did he know something she didn't? "What ya got, HP? Com'on give."

"How about if I told you the someone who knows someone is the janitor-bot at the League's main propulsion research lab, and she tells me Herman talks about you all the time?"

"She? Is this janitor-bot your girl-bot friend?"

Hushpuppy regarded her in silence for several seconds. She sensed he was embarrassed. Finally the bot said, "How about I arrange for a double date at the HSB outlet two blocks over for tomorrow night—you, me and my friend, and Herman?"

Trixie thought for a minute. She had to eat anyway, that was mandatory, and she'd meet HP's girl-bot friend, which would be as cool as lettuce, and she'd see an old friend of hers too. She shrugged, "Sure, why not. It'll be fun to catch up with Herman."

"Great. Leave the arrangements to me. What time do you usually have your second dinner?"

"Always at five thirty," Trixie said. Keeping to a regular feeding schedule was important to her.

***

True to his word, at five twenty-five precisely, Hushpuppy arrived in an air taxi outside her apartment to accompany her to the restaurant. After Trixie was loaded by the driver-bot into the rear seat, and her hover chair was stored on the magnetic roof pad, they were off.

By her calculations she'd be seated at five thirty precisely with her first order of double-double cheeseburger, mega-fries, and a half gallon lime and cola soda in front of her ten seconds before the first hunger pang was due to start.

It was always close, but she'd learned the hard way, when her mother once withheld a meal as punishment, what hunger felt like, and the experience was so terrible she didn't want to ever feel even one pang again. Eating at five forty-five had been so awful it was seared into her memory forever.

The taxi stopped in front of the Quarter Pound Street HSB location at five twenty seven, right on schedule. They were seated at a four-hover-chair table at five twenty nine. Trixie had of course sent an e-order on the way, so at five thirty exactly the food arrived in front of her.

The waiter-bot brought the credit scanner, which he held out for her to see, the screen with the total.

13

Part 1

As usual they had rounded the total up to the nearest hundred credits.

Trixie abhorred the practice, knowing it made them the only fast food chain in the galaxy who still practiced rounding up. She'd often mused that when she was in charge there'd be no more rounding up at the burger bar. It was no mystery to her why they were 151st of 152 on Food E-Zine's Annual List of Most Successful Fast Food Chains. She pressed her thumb on the scanner's screen to authorize the payment.

Her mouth watered as she gazed at her food.

Looking around, she saw the restaurant was crowded with diners chewing and tearing into burgers, fries, and deep fried goodies of all kinds. Trixie didn't see Herman or HP's girl-bot friend anywhere.

It was nearly thirty seconds after five thirty. She scowled at Hushpuppy, who sat passively across from her with a bowl of lubricating oil in front of him.

She decided not to wait for them and began to eat. She picked up the burger in her meaty fingers; it dripped greasy juices down her arms. Trixie stuffed the sandwich into her mouth and tore a huge chunk out and began to chew loudly.

"Where are they?" She mumbled between bites.

"I'm not going to go hungry, because I get grumpy when I'm hungry. And you wouldn't like me when I'm grumpy."

"Hey, Trix, how's tricks," said a deep male voice she recognized from behind her.

She set her burger on the plate and turned her hover chair around to face him. She smiled when she saw it was indeed Herman Pug. She gazed into his gray-blue eyes, feeling drawn in by his handsome features. He even had those same black framed glasses balanced on the tip of his narrow nose, and he hadn't changed out of his white lab coat. It amused her to think it was the same coat he'd worn while at school.

"Hi, Herm, it's really good to see you." Trixie realized she was gushing. How embarrassing, but I can't help myself. I really like this guy.

Herman grabbed a nearby chair kept for customers without hover chairs and sat across from her. His lips curled up at one corner, and he had a lock of black hair that had fallen across the top of his pale forehead.

Before Trixie could say anything the female janitor-bot rushed up to the table and hovered next to Hushpuppy. "Sorry I'm late, everyone. I had a toilet emergency and had to get it done before I could leave.

Trixie was pleased the bot hadn't elaborated since she had her food already. A toilet emergency for a bot, who had no digestive system, was very different from a human.

"Everyone," said Hushpuppy, "This is Tri-Top, my fiancé. We're getting married."

Trixie chocked on the fries she'd stuffed into her mouth, some were hanging outside her mouth and almost fell. She spat them across the table and glared at HP. Married? He picks now to spring this on me? I'm here meeting a man I've had a crush on for a decade who I haven't seen in a year, and he surprises us with this!

Herman seemed unfazed by HP's sudden announcement. "Well, isn't that great. Let me buy dinner to celebrate."

Trixie smiled sheepishly. "Huh, I already paid for mine, Herm."

Herman waved off her objection. "No worries. I'll get the waiter to add on your bill to the total for the table and refund yours."

"Yeah. OK." Trixie knew the restaurant would refund her the amount before the rounding up. then round up his bill. This way HSB would make money at both ends of the transaction. She really had to do something about this policy.

Ripping off customers was just plain wrong.

"You guys wanta be at the wedding?" said Hushpuppy, his tone excited. You could even both be in the wedding party."

Trixie eyed HP, "As what?"

"Well, Tri-Top and I talked about it, and you are my best human friend, Trixie, so we'd like you to be Tri's human maid of honor." (As required by the Robot Marriage Act of 2998 all robots who marry must have a human best man and maid of honor to make the marriage legal. There were a few bots who lived in common-law relationships, but they were mostly home appliance-bots.)

Trixie looked to Herman, her beady eyes pleading for help. "I think that would be a great idea," said Herman.

Oh, brother, can this get any worse?

"And, Herman, I know we just met, but since you're such a good friend of Trixie's how about you be the human best man?"

Oh, shoot me now.

Part 2

Calories are meant to be consumed, not counted. — Galactic Food Guide for Maximum Health 370th edition, page 4902, paragraph 3, copyright 2952

HERMAN FIDGETED AND PULLED AT THE COLLAR of his tuxedo jumpsuit. Trixie glared at him indicating he should stop. Since he was standing next to her in the chapel behind the bride and grooming listening to the auto-preacher droning on about how commitments between two bots was a significant symbol for all robot kind. Trixie rolled her eyes. Blah, blah, blah.

She frowned and moved her hover chair closer to Herman and gently bumped the front edge against his knee. He winced and looked at her his eyes wide with surprise. He rubbed his knee vigorously.

"What?" he whispered.

"Stop fidgeting this is a wedding."

Not that Trixie was thrilled herself to be the maid of honor at Hushpuppy and Tripod's wedding. Robot weddings were soooo long, they wouldn't eat for at least half an hour yet. And the robot chapel was so hot at this time of day. Trixie glanced at the digital clock in the arm of her chair. The time was 11:45, fifteen minutes until her third meal of the day and she knew it would be late.

Of course what really bugged her was that she'd been tricked into serving as the human maid of honor at this wedding. All she really ever wanted was a nice lunch with Hushpuppy (aka HP), and Tripod and their friend, Herman Pug. HP told her Herman had some new space ship engine drive that could rocket her up the Heavenly Sky Burger promotional ladder far ahead of schedule. (Secretly she hoped they didn't expect her to climb a real ladder, she was afraid of heights). If Herman's star drive was all HP said it was she could be the head deep fry cook at the Heaven Sky Burger store she worked at by next week. She was disappointed her Hamburger University degree hadn't landed her a plum position from day one.

Her boss, Mr. Pickles-On-The-Side, said she had to prove herself before her next promotion, but she hoped Herman would be just what she needed to roll her hover chair up the ladder.

Part 2

But Herman was a skinny. Too skinny a skinny at that. She glanced at him standing next to her with his sweaty hands, and ill-fitting tuxedo jumpsuit. She rolled her eyes then looked straight ahead again and tried to block out the drone of the robot pastor's marriage speech.

Like all skinnies no doubt Herman had trouble finding clothes for the weight challenged. (Her mother always insisted she use the PC term rather the street slang her and her friends in high school used. Skinny drips and picky eaters were favorite targets.)

His baggy tux certainly supported her hypothesis. But there was something about him she liked. They'd been through the rehearsal dinners, practice lunches, and after coffee snacks, Herman actually seemed a little flesher in the face. He was obviously trying to impress her. And his deep brown eyes revealed a depth reminiscent of dark chocolate.

Hmmmm.....dark chocolate. Her stomach grumbled and her mouth began to water at the mental image of a chocolate bar floating on a mash mellow cloud. She closed her eyes to stop the room from spinning. If she didn't eat soon she'd faint from hunger.

She blinked repeatedly and shifted her numb bottom on her chair.

Her ruminations had come to an abrupt end as Pastor Oilcan said the final words, "I now pronounce you robot-husband and robot-wife, mated until your power cells drain of the last of their energy." Since bot's power cells were designed to last for a thousand years these two were really in this marriage thing for the long haul.

I hope I never make such a huge mistake.

The chapel was filled to capacity with guests, and family, and a group of bot mechanics from Bill's Robot Garage. The patch over their left breast pockets flashed the name of the garage repeatedly nearly blinding her when she first spotted them in the back pew near the twin doors leading to the dining hall. She'd been looking for the emergency exit in case the protestors outside managed to break through the police blockade when she spotted the three human women seated at the back.

Trice was relieved they were smiling. This meant they were progressive thinkers and not party to the protest marches going on outside the chapel. Even in this day and age there were still humans who considered bot-marriage wrong.

Trixie couldn't believe some of the neon signs attached to their hover chairs.

'What's next human-bot marriage?' or 'My toaster loves me.' or even the absurd, 'I'd rather marry my cheeseburger.' That last one did actually make sense to Trixie. But then she'd always loved food more than people.

Her mouth began to water at the thought of the copious quantities of burgers and fried foods that waited for her on the other side of those doors.

(The Robot Marriage Act requires all robot weddings to have sufficient food for ten servings per human attendee. Failure to provide this minimum number of servings will result in automatic draining of power cells of all robot attendees and the support bots.)

Finally the ceremony ended and the procession started moving down the aisle. Wayyy too slowly as far as Trixie was concerned, but after what seemed like forever the matching doors to the reception room finally slid into the doorframe. Trixie's eyes went wide and her heart rate increased.

Before them was a plethora of fresh hot burgers and fries on a long, long table in the center of the room. Through teary eyes that blurred her vision Trixie could see the three-milkshake machines at the end of the long tables of food. She sighed inwardly.

It was as if she'd died and been buried in the Tomb of the Unknown Customer.

"Like that would ever happen," she mused.

"You say something?" asked Herman.

She wiped at her eyes with the back of a chubby hand then offered him a weak smile. "Just dreaming big," she said and sniffled.

Herman smiled. "We all dream big," he whispered reassuringly.

"Let's eat," she said wanting to change the subject. Not that this was difficult since the first pangs of hunger had begun to creep up from her stomach.

He nodded and shrugged.

***

After five hours of eating Trixie finally felt satisfied. She sighed as she loosened the hover chair's seatbelt a notch by pressing the button on the control panel recessed in the right arm. Trixie looked over at Herman and saw he was leaned back in his chair looking surprisingly ill for someone who'd just eaten his share of the wonderful, greasy feast before them.

Frankly it surprised her when he took so many burgers and fries at round one. For a skinny he could really chow down. She had grown a new respect for him and his ability to eat. He seemed eager to please. She smiled to herself. Herman had real potential.

Part 2

But now she would have an intimate and really important discussion with him to determine if he was the right man for her.

"Herman, tell me a little about this new space drive you've invented." Herman's eyes were slits and he groaned as he turned his head slightly to face her. "Herman? Are you okay?" Her heart began to race. Maybe he had food poisoning. Maybe she'd been poisoned too!

No! She couldn't miss a single day at the Heavenly Sky Burger outlet where she worked as a once-a-day-floor-mop-swiper. If she missed even one day this early in her career it would end her dream of absolute dominance of the burger chain before it started. And her dream of ending the rounding up at the burger bar that went on far too much. This was her mission, that and to make HSB the number one fast food chain in the galaxy of course.

Herman's mouth hung open and drool ran out one side and down his chin. "Did I really have to eat everything?" he mumbled.

She looked at him aghast. "Eat what? All you've eaten is one serving; five burgers, three large fries, and two milkshakes. That's nothing. And I was forced to eat a portion of your serving to cover up your lack of gluttony.

"For goodness sake suck it up, man."

"You don't understand," he said. "I've never eaten this much food in one sitting, ever." He groaned.

"Shhhhh...." Trixie looked around and saw a few people were staring at them. Oh, crap, I better get him outta here before we're both embarrassed. Especially me.

"Com'on, let's glide our way outta here like spent fryer grease."

"Makes sense to me," agreed Herman with a nod and a weak grin.

***

They arrived at Herman's lab at the university in a hover cab. It was late but Trixie wasn't worried about being late for work the next day. Mr. Pickles-On-The-Side was due to be on vacation for the next two weeks. He was off to a fat farm, lucky old creep. He was probably going to gain as much as twenty pounds. One day, she thought wistfully, I'll have enough credits to go on such a luxury vacation. When I'm CEO I'll buy six fat farms and visit them any time I want.

Herman wobbled out of the hover cab while Trixie pressed her thumb on the payment pad to cover the fare. It was a days wages but worth it if what she had in mind paid off.

Part 2

Herman walked to the door to the lab and mumbled the code. The door slid aside with a loud swoosh sound startling Trixie. What the heck was that?

Trixie floated her chair until she was beside Herman. "Does the door always make that sound?"

Herman nodded. "Burpppp. Uhhh, yeah, it was Mickey's idea. He heard it in a 20th century movie vid. He thought it was a neat sound so I programmed the door to make a swoosh every time it opens and closes."

Trixie nodded then rolled her eyes when he turned away from her.

"Lights," he said before entering the open door. The lights came on and Trixie froze where she stood when she saw what was beyond.

A burger-shaped object at least six feet across filled the room. In fact it looked exactly like a burger, a top and bottom bun, a piece of glistening meat, golden ribbons of melted cheese frozen in mid-drip down the sides of the meat.

Though she'd eaten her last meal only an hour ago her mouth filled with saliva. Her heart pounded rapidly in her ears. This was the most delicious sight she had ever seen. A hamburger this size produced on a massive scale would solve the galaxy's burger shortages.

Finally she took in a breath and the odor of fuel invaded her senses immediately souring her stomach. "What the heck?" she breathed. It wasn't real, it was burger shaped, but it wasn't a burger.

She floated through the door and it closed behind her as soon as she cleared the doorway. Now she was worried. I'm trapped.

"Hey, babe, what's happenin'?" said a deep male voice.

Trixie turned her chair to the right then to the left. No one was there.

"Up here, babe," said the voice.

Trixie leaned back and then she saw it. A vaguely half-moon shaped slug-like alien was floating on gossamer wings near the ceiling. There were no visible orifices breaking its smooth purple skin. Its shape and color reminded her of an eggplant before it was properly deep-fried.

The only fast food chain serving eggplant was The Double Deep Fry Clubhouse. She'd only been there once, but soon tired of deep fried vegetables. Vegetables were so unhealthy.

But how did the alien talk to her with no mouth? And how did it see her?

"Ummm, Herman, what is that?"

Part 2

The flying purple slug floated closer to her. "Hey, lady! I'm not a that!"

Herman had his back to Trixie but now he turned around and his eyes went wide as he watched the purple alien getting ever closer to Trixie. "Whoa! Hold on Mickey!"

The slug stopped and hovered above her. "But Herman she was rude."

The corners of Herman's mouth curled slightly upward and his eyes sparkled. "I'm pretty certain Trixie has never met a Purple before."

Trixie shook her head and backed her chair up so she could see the flying alien without having to stretch her neck back so far. "You're right, I've never even seen one before." Trixie paused and realized she better address the slug directly. It may not have a mouth or teeth or claws but it still might be able to hurt her. How she had no idea, but why take the chance?

"Uhhh...Mickey is it?"

"Mickelott actually," said the alien.

Trixie looked to Herman who explained. "Mickelott Pug was my great, great, grandfather the inventor of the ice cream jet. Mickey's real name is unpronounceable by human vocal chords so I call him Mickelott." He shrugged. "He doesn't mind. Right, Mickey?"

"Of course not, Herman.   You're my best friend."

Herman's best friend is a flying purple slug reminiscent of a (she shuddered) vegetable? I'll have to fix that as soon as I can if I want Herman to help me with my plan. And I thought aliens had a non-interference rule they had to follow. She shook off her revulsion. "How did you two meet?" asked Trixie.

"Herman rescued me from my home world, Marzipan Two," explained Mickey

Trixie cocked any eyebrow at Herman whose cheeks flushed crimson. "Well, not exactly. I adopted him when I was ten years old."

"Same thing," sniffed Mickey.

Trixie shook her head. "I'm confused."

Herman sighed and his shoulders slumped. "Do you remember that breakfast cereal they used to sell, Super Sugar Bombs?"

She nodded. "Certainly. It was replaced by New Improvised Super Sugar Bombs with ten times the sugary goodness." Her heart beat faster as she realized what he meant. "Didn't they have a coupon in every box for an adopt an alien program?"

Herman avoided her eyes, hanging his head, he nodded. "Yes," he said softly.

"But if I recall correctly you had to collect ten thousand coupons..." Her voice trailed off when she realized the implications of what she was saying. Her eyes went wide and her mouth began to water. She swallowed the additional saliva then continued. "There was a scandal just before the manufacturer declared bankruptcy, and the new improved version was bought out by another company, which was much better by the way."

Herman's eyes were wide. "How do you know all this?"

Trixie grinned. "First year at Hamburger U I took a class in Pitfalls and Mistakes of the Food Corporations and How To Avoid Them. We did a case study of the major cereal companies. One company was Ajax Foods who used to make Sugar Bombs."

Herman grunted. "Wow, you have some memory."

Trixie's brow wrinkled. "I seem to recall there was only one person who managed to collect enough coupons to adopt an alien." She looked at Herman. "You?" He nodded. "But how did you eat so much cereal? I don't mean to offend but you're so skinny."

Herman chucked. "No offense taken. The body you see before you now used to weight two hundred pounds more. I lost weight when I became a propulsion research scientist. Too much time in the laboratory, and not enough at the dining table." He grinned.

Trixie smiled weakly, but inside she was horrified to think of anyone who neglected food in favor of work. Normally you can't trust people who make food second in their lives, but she had grown so fond of Herman she was prepared to ignore his lack of beauty fat, and his eating habits.

Someone had to help him, he was obviously so helpless without someone with her skills and education. It was then she made up her mind. One day she'd marry Herman Pug and save him from himself.

Trixie watched the Purple lay on top of the hamburger shaped engine. After it settled it's wings lay flat against its shiny body. "Well, then it's nice to meet you, Mickelott."

"You too, babe," replied the purple alien. "Since you're a friend of Herman's you can call me Mickey."

Cheeky bugger.

Part 2

But Herman was friends with Mickey so she'd have to make it appear she was willing to be friends with the Purple until she could 86 him from Herman's life.

Trixie moved her chair closer to the burger engine. "This is sure cool looking—for an engine. Tell me more about it."

"I don't know..." Herman began.

"Hey, why not, Herman, Trixie is a friend after all," said Mickey.

Trixie smiled at the purple alien still atop the giant burger engine. Maybe he wasn't so bad after all. He appeared to have some influence over the scientist so she might be able to use that.

She was after all considered a hottie and a good catch since she worked at a fast food chain that had nowhere to go but up. Being one hundred and fifty first out of one hundred and fifty two fast food companies in the galaxy meant there was a long way to go to reach the number one spot. Good thing burgers were beginning to overtake pizza in popularity once again.

A sour taste filled Trixie's mouth at the thought of pizza. Vile stuff, with a vegetable based tomato sauce, and small circles of meat on a flour disc. Yuck! Small meat? Awful.

Once she became CEO she'd remove the rounding up policy, and change the special sauce recipe, and then everyone would see Heavenly Sky Burger become number one. Trixie mentally rubbed her hands together in glee at the thought. And Herman Pug would be the man behind the powerful woman.

But right now she had to make ooh and ahhh sounds about some smelly old engine.

"So what does it do?" she asked, not that she was at all interested.

Herman smiled and his eyes sparkled with a fever and energy she'd not seen in him until now. "It's a new star drive that will revolutionize travel in the galaxy and allow the user to expand their markets faster than ever before."

Now he got her attention. "How?"

Herman launched into an explanation, parts of which she didn't understand, but the gist of which was this new propulsion drive would allow a Marketeer ship to traverse to the edge of the galaxy in two weeks versus the two years it took now.

This meant the supply lines to the outer world stores would no longer be delayed as often as occurred today. And it would mean the fleets could seek out new markets and new suppliers far faster than ever before.

Now they could boldly go where no fast food chain had ever gone before.

Trixie felt her cheeks grow cold as the blood drained from her face. She shivered.

If HSB controlled this engine they would quickly become number one, and she as the discoverer of the greatest propulsion scientist in the universe, would rise quickly to the heights she deserved. Wow!

She had to have the engine no matter what the cost. "Ummm, Herman, who owns the patent to the engine?"

Herman looked at her and his brow wrinkled. "Zippy Piner's family paid for the research. I'm just a poor scientist so I couldn't have made the break through I did without their generous grants."

Trixie smiled sweetly. "Yes, but who owns the patents?"

Herman nodded. "Me."

"Good." Trixie fought the urge to rub her hands together in glee.

That's when Mickey spoke up. "Herman's engaged to Zippy."

Trixie's jaw dropped. Oh, crap. Now what?

Part 3

Grease makes the world go around. And keeps your pants up. And fuels the economy. — Bacon Sample, Director General of the Galactic Central Bank speaking at the Heavenly Sky Burger Annual Franchisee Convention to a standing ovation

Trixie's hover chair was parked beside the dishwasher station where Cherry Bomb worked hard pushing buttons to start and stop the automatic dishwasher. Someday I'll invent the button-free automatic dishwasher.

"Say, Cherry, do you like your job?"

Cherry held a large plasti-steel pot by both handles.

Trixie sighed.

Part 3

The retired security specialist had four arms, so she could get her job done in half the time it took Trixie to make her one swipe with the floor mop per shift.

When Trixie asked her question, one of Cherry's two heads turned to face her while the other stayed concentrating on the pot now sunk into a tub of soapy water.

"Why do you ask?" said the four-limbed, two-headed, four-eyed alien. Her skin color was representative of her name.

Trixie shrugged. "I don't know. It's just that I'm made for better things than being a floor swiper at the 152nd most popular fast food chain."

"Have you completed your single mop swipe for today?" Cherry asked.

Trixie's brow wrinkled, and she arched an eyebrow at her friend. "Since when did they make you the manager?"

Cherry's eyes went wide, and she turned her second head to face the pot that two of her hands were scrubbing with a long handled pot scrubber. The smell of rich cheese sauce and detergent wafted over Trixie. Her nose wrinkled at the scent of the lavender soap while her stomach growled at the smell of the cheese. She pushed away the sudden wave of hunger. It was at least ten minutes until her next meal.

As her mother used to say when Trixie still lived at home, 'Eight meals a day make a girl fat and sassy for love.' Truthfully, Trixie had no idea what her mother meant, but it sure sounded interesting. She had no time for love, not when she had her sights on the greasy corporate ladder.

"Aioli!"

Oh, crap! It was Mr. Pickles On The Side! He must be right behind me. I am soooo fired.

Cherry was no help. She turned her attention back to the pot, and the water began to splash up the sides of the plasti-steel tub as she rubbed harder.

Trixie manipulated the controls on the arm of her chair, and the chair turned her to face her red-faced, blood-shot-eyed, very angry boss. (actually, Mr. POTS' race always had blood-shot eyes, so this wasn't unusual.) She broke into the widest smile she could manage. Her cheeks actually hurt. Smiling was not her forté.

"Uhhh, Mr. Pickles On The Side? Sir, I'm so pleased to see you."

Mr. POTS scowled, and his face actually turned an even deeper shade of crimson. He cocked one eyebrow. "Really, Aioli? Really?" He snorted. "I hardly think so. I just checked your mop, and it's dry. Can you explain to me why it's dry?"

Part 3

"Ummm, well, sir ... you see —"

"No worries, Mr. POTS, I dried it for her."

Cherry? What the heck was she doing? We're both gonna get fired, and it'll be my fault.

Mr. POTS looked doubtful, but his scowl eased to a frown. Finally his features gradually relaxed. "Oh," was all he said. He then turned away and floated toward his office on his hover cycle.

Trixie eyed her retreating manager with envy. He had enough credits for a hover flyer. These were new on the market and all the movers and shakers and rollers were replacing their hover chairs with these streamlined, sleek machines. A sudden sharp pain in the pit of her stomach snapped her back to reality.

Cherry stopped washing the cooking pot she'd been working on and let it sink into the soapy water. She snatched a hand towel off the rail that ran around the edge of the plasti-steel sink and began to dry her two wet hands. "Hungry?" she asked.

"Uhhh, yeah." Trixie glanced at the digital time display recessed into her chair arm. "Of course." It was ten minutes to meal break. (The Galactic Law Review of 3123 recommended all employees have a minimum of five meal breaks per six-hour shift.

The recommendation became law in 3222 after it was determined fast food employers allowed six meal breaks per six hour shift anyway.)

Cherry threw the wet towel into the laundry hamper next to the dishwashing station. It would be launched into space with the garbage. She then joined Trixie walking beside her chair. Together, they headed for the employee dining hall. (This always unnerved Trixie because the ex-security specialist towered over her. Trixie sometimes wondered if she had tall-o-phobia.)

Cherry opened the door to the employee dining room, and Trixie floated through on her chair.

It seemed to Trixie her chair was moving sluggishly. The nuclear battery must be running low. Since she'd had the same chair since she was twelve, it wasn't surprising. She'd have to pay a visit to the hover chair service station after work and get it checked.

The dining hall could seat more than a hundred employees. By law, every fast food outlet had to provide enough space to hold the annual employee food meeting and party- down-like-an-animal eater fest. (Annual, meaning every month — Galactic New Dictionary, copyright 2899.)

Tables stretched from four feet in front the door across the cavernous room. A podium with a lectern was against the far wall. One wall was comprised of floor to ceiling smoked glass windows overlooking the street where people in hover chairs went by.

The street was filled with hover cabs and hover cycles. Robot janitors holding long handled electric brooms swept the sidewalk as the people tossed food wrappers to the ground as they went by. It was a typical street scene — one that could be found in every city on Dirt, and on many more planets throughout the galaxy.

There were only four empty tables left in the dining hall, but at least they were near the door. The others were occupied by other employees on duty during the day shift. Trixie was proud she'd scored a spot on the day shift; only the fattest employees got one of the coveted spots.

She spotted Twinkie McFry seated with the assistant to the assistant of the assistant manager. She waved, and he acknowledged her with a tight smile and a nod, then went back to chewing his fried chicken.

Trixie knew the Twink was sucking up again, but if Trixie managed to invent (steal, actually, because why invent when it was easier to steal and take credit? Inventing was hard work.) something spectacular, then she'd out-climb not only Twink, but also every other wannabe manager in the place.

Once Trixie and Cherry were seated at a table, the robot waiter appeared. While he looked human (more so than Cherry), he wasn't. He walked to the table, for one thing. No self-respecting Dirter would ever walk when you could ride on a hover chair or hover cycle. And then there were the eyes. Sure his eyes didn't smile but they were dreamy bedroom eyes. Her heart skipped a beat as his eyes paused to gaze upon her. She felt like an under deep fried potato, all limp and wilty.

Regardless, this one was called Tip Top, and he certainly was a cutie and a darn good waiter. His designer had a good eye for detail. Wavy dark hair, eyes the color of sea-blue, and a square jaw with a dimple at the tip. Oooo-la-la, did he come out of the factory ready-made for a snuggle.

"Miss Trixie. How nice to see you again," Tip said as he placed the menus on the table.

Of course they came in here every day, and every day Tip said the same thing.

Part 3

Not that Trixie didn't' enjoy the attention. "Thanks, Tip, it's nice to see you as well."

"The usual, Miss Trixie?" He always placed the menu in front of her and always asked her if she wanted her usual. A triple cheese burger with the mountain-o-fries and extra large grape soda. Meal three was always the same. But today Trixie felt adventurous.

"No, Tip, I think I'll have the onion rings instead of the fries."

Tip chuckled and picked up the menu from in front of Trixie. "Excellent choice, Miss Trixie, chef cut the onions fresh this morning. Mountain style, naturally?" Trixie grinned and nodded. "But of course."

Tip shifted his gaze to Cherry. "And you, Miss Cherry?"

"I'll have the usual."

Trixie's stomach became slightly queasy. Cherry only ate fried-eel sandwiches, breakfast 1 and 2; lunch 1, 2, and 3; and dinner 1, 2, 3, and 4. No matter how many times she saw her friend eat fried eels it still made her stomach unsettled.

At least it's fried, she thought. I only hope they never run out of eels.

It was a good thing HSB cornered the eel market by making first contact (and first contract) with Slippery IV in the Ophis Nebula where Cherry's home planet, Slippery III, orbited a giant red star in the same system.

"Very good, Miss Cherry."

It amazed Trixie how Tip could make every order sound like the smartest order ever.

After Tip left to deliver their orders to the kitchen, Cherry cleared her throat. Trixie shifted her gaze to her friend. She knew that throat clearing well. "What is it?"

Cherry looked away. "What about Herman?"

Trixie tensed. Yes, what about Herman? He was engaged to be married to Zippy Piner and be drawn into a pizza family. And worst of all the new engine he'd invented would derive any fast food's marketeer fleet of intergalactic ships farther, and faster than ever in history. Trixie dreamed the new FTL technology Herman developed would be owned, copyrighted, patented, and trademarked by Heavenly Sky Burger. And she'd be in the big chair, the CEO controlling it all. No star system or planet would slip between her greasy fingers.

Part 3

As far as she was concerned the board of directors at HSB were driving the company to ruin by not stopping the impending marriage of Herman Pug. She'd even sent an anonymous message to the current CEO, but she'd never responded. Cool Whipper Butterscotch might have been the greatest CEO of the last twenty years, and she had patented the double ice cream deep fry, but she'd run out of fresh ideas.

Trying to appear casual in front of her friend she shrugged while keeping her eyes focused on the empty table. Normally she didn't like to look at a table without food on it, but she had to concentrate so as not to let on she was deeply disappointed Herman was marrying someone else. She needed his technology if she was going to take over Heavenly Sky Burger.

"When's the wedding?" she said.

"This weekend. Saturday. Three o'clock."

"That's nice."

Before Cherry heaped any more discomfort on her, Tip Top appeared with their orders. Just in time too. The waiter-bot set down the burger and fries platter in front of her. Cherry disappeared behind the mountain of onion rings. Trixie wouldn't see her again until half the delicious, oily rings of batter-coated deep-golden-brown onions were consumed.

Trixie's mouth watered as she gazed at the mound of glistening onion rings beside the thick stack of perfectly cooked burgers, the melted cheese dripping down the sides of the meat onto the platter.

"Will there be anything else, Miss Aioli?" asked Tip Top.

Trixie stole a glance at Tip then locked her gaze on the delicious food. Herman had been forgotten, at least for the moment. "No, I think that'll be it for now, Tip. But come back in ten minutes with a soda refill. OK?"

"Surely," replied the waiter-bot before disappearing once again.

After ten minutes Trixie had worked her way through the rings to the level where she could see Cherry eating the last of her deep-fried eel. Cherry burped, a sign of perfectly cooked eel. One side of Trixie's mouth curled upward.

"You wanna stop the wedding?"

Trixie almost choked on the hunk of burger, cheese, mayo, and bun she'd just stuffed in her mouth. "What?" she mumbled around her food.

"Are you interested in preventing the wedding of Herman to Zippy?" Cherry said, being more specific this time.

Part 3

Trixie felt a knot of excitement form in the pit of her stomach. What was her friend talking about? "Let's say I'm interested. How exactly would I do that?"

Cherry looked up from her food, her black eyes locked on Trixie's. "I have a friend of a friend who has a time machine."

Trixie swallowed the food in her mouth and stared across the cooling onion rings at Cherry. "A time machine?" She fought the urge to burst out laughing. The biggest brains in the galaxy had been trying to conquer time travel since they broke the FTL barrier almost a thousand years ago.

Sure FTL travel was a form of time travel with the time delineation involved, but no one as far as she knew had ever managed to travel back in time. Or to the future as far as anyone could tell. Besides time travel was made illegal when it suddenly dawned on someone a smart fast food executive could manipulate time to their advantage.

Trixie loved the danger aspect of what Cherry was suggesting. She craved to know more. "Tell me about your friend."

***

At the end of their shift, Cherry ordered a hover cab to take them to her friend's home on the outskirts of Cheesetown.

Trixie sat beside Cherry growing increasingly worried as they traveled farther and farther past the houses and fast food outlets.

When the discount outlets such as Econo-Dog and The Soft Ice Cream Budget Warehouse appeared Trixie knew they'd arrived in the bad part of town. The locals moving along the sidewalks had the oldest models of hover chairs, and not the collectible kind either. These chairs were the shabbily made imports from the rim worlds, made by aliens with little understanding of humanoid requirements. Even her chair was custom-made for her girth and could be easily adjusted as she hopefully gained weight.

This area of town was known to frequented by gangs of food rebels. There was even a rumor that a vegetarian lived out here. Trixie shuddered at the thought of anyone with vegetables as a sole source of their food. Poison. Radicals.

Finally the cab came to a stop outside a dilapidated house that appeared to be at least five hundred years old or more. The house sagged to the right as if it were a lean-to. The color of the plasti-steel had clearly faded from its original fire-engine red to a pale red. Most houses were repainted every year, but this one hadn't been touch in a long time.

"Where are we?" Trixie breathed.

Part 3

The bot cab driver answered before Cherry did. "Pont l'Eveque."

Oh crap. Pont l'Eveque was the galaxy's stinkiest cheese. Now she was afraid to get out of the hover cab.

"Let's go ," said Cherry. "This is Graham's place."

"Your friend lives here?" Trixie shook her head but got out, her hover chair carrying her out the door to the sidewalk. She almost got back in the cab when the smell of the stinky cheese that permeated the air struck her in the nostrils with full force. For the first time in her life she was within a hair's width of losing her appetite.

Cherry, seeing Trixie's discomfort, handed her a small white pill. "What's this?"

"A pill that will deaden your sense of smell until we leave here."

Trixie glared at the four-limbed alien. "I have two questions: Will I be able to smell my food after we leave here? 100% guaranteed? And two: Will this awful smell go away?"

She glanced around at the people passing them by on the sidewalk. Their eyes were sunken and dull. She thought they looked thinner than those in the other parts of the city.

Smell was a very important sense when it came to enjoying food.

Cherry shrugged. "The answer to your first question is the manufacturer guarantee states the pills effects will dissipate within an hour, and to your second question, yes the smell will go away, but we will have to burn our clothes and have long showers when we get home." Cherry paused while Trixie popped the pill in her mouth then leaned toward the straw that appeared from her chair arm to the cola flavored soda in the chair's storage tank. She took a long swig of the soda to ensure the pill went down.

Within a few seconds the smell of the dreadful cheese disappeared. Thank the God's of Perfectly Fried Foods. She breathed deeply and was pleased when no odiferous odors invaded her senses.

"The people who live around here take these pills by the bushel. C'mon, let's go." Cherry started up the winding path of irregular stones to the front door of the sad little house where someone named Graham lived.

Odd name, thought Trixie. Her chair carried her after Cherry, who was quickly speaking into the vid phone next to the door. Trixie smiled to herself. She'd half expected an ancient sound-only com unit given the house's condition.

Part 3

A round face the color of sun-baked wheat appeared on the view screen. With three eyes, the pupils royal purple, and the bushy orange hair on his round head, Graham was clearly not human.

"C'mon in, Cherry. And bring Trix with ya." The alien wiggled his three blond eyebrows suggestively.

Trixie rolled her eyes after the screen went dark. Oh, brother. He's gonna hit on me. She sighed to herself. What's a girl to do when she's as hot as a fresh jalapeno?

The door swung inward, and they entered.

The inside of the house was far more modern than the exterior. The walls were banana yellow with red trim along the edges. The furniture was modern in style and taste and along one wall was a massive vid screen that filled the entire wall.

This guy must do well at whatever he does. Actually it's a very nice place.

The alien who appeared in the door vid phone appeared in his hover chair from a hallway. Trixie swallowed hard as her mouth dried of any remnants of moisture. The pill not only killed her sense of smell, but taste as well. This alien — Graham — was one handsome specimen in his brand new 3303 model year hover chair.

Obviously this Graham was a being of money, good taste, and devastating good looks. She would have to be on her guard around him. Her mission was to stop Herman from marrying Zippy, and marry him herself. Then she'd gain control of the new star drive, use it to expand the HSB brand, and become CEO of the number one fast food franchise in the galaxy.

"Hey, Cherry, good to see ya!" Graham's voice was husky, and the reverberation seemed to cut through her.

"You too, Graham," said Cherry with a smile in her tone. Cherry turned slightly toward Trixie. "Graham Wafers, I'd like you to meet Trixie Aioli, the best floor swiper at Heavenly Sky Burger."

Graham's wide mouth formed a toothy smile. "It's a pleasure, Miss Aioli."

"For me as well, Mr. Wafers." She arched one eyebrow. "Are you of the Toaster-Tart II Wafers, by any chance?"

Not that she knew anyone of that wealthy family, but she read the society blogs every day and made it a point to name drop whenever the opportunity arose. You never knew who you might meet, and have to impress.

Part 3

Graham chuckled, his heavy jowls jiggling and making Trixie aroused and hungry simultaneously. "No, I'm afraid not." The smile faded from his features, and his eyes narrowed. "I understand you want to time travel to stop a wedding?" His eyes flitted to Cherry, who nodded.

"Yes," Trixie added so as not to give the perception that this was Cherry's mission, not hers and hers alone.

Graham nodded grimly. "You do know what your asking is illegal?" Trixie nodded. "And that if we're caught we'll be sentenced to hard time at a fat farm?"

Trixie nodded again. If they were caught, farming fat was the least of her worries.

Graham stole one last glance at Cherry, who remained silent, then looked back to Trixie. "OK. But there are rules."

"Like what?" asked Trixie.

"You can only travel to the past, and then only six weeks back. Maximum." He paused. "Will this work for you?"

Trixie's lips formed a smile. "I don't care about any stinking rules. I want this. Badly. And I'm willing to pay."

A sardonic grin spread across Graham's handsome features. "Oh, believe me, you'll pay."

Trixie's heart beat hard in her chest and the excitement knot had returned in the pit of her stomach. This is gonna be fun. Besides what's the worst that can happen?

Part 4

Question 13,423 - If it takes sixty burgers to complete a marathon how many does it take to screw in a light bulb?
— Page 3467, The Big Book of Interesting Food Questions, 493rd Edition, copyright 2995

WHEN TRIXIE WOKE UP THIS MORNING — the wedding day of the man she wanted to marry, who was marrying someone else — she never thought she'd find herself time traveling to the past to save her future.

But she was now six weeks ago standing up to her ankles in a pool of rain water. Her slip-on flats wet, and her feet cold as if they were submerged in her favorite grape flavored slushy drink.

She gritted her teeth and stepped out of the puddle. The shoe auto dry feature immediately activated and quickly dried her shoes. Too bad her socks didn't have this feature.

She winced as she moved her left foot and the cold water soaked into her socks sloshed inside her shoe.

Trixie looked at the time and date on the wrist chronometer Graham Wafers had given her to wear and saw she had indeed traveled to the past. Exactly six weeks in the past to be exact...

Oh, for the love of fries my inner voice is repeating itself. I hope I'm not stuck in a causality loop.

Bu then she still suffered from a bit of a chill from the walk in freezer-slash-closet slash-time travel machine she and Cherry had come through to get to the here and now.

Her stomach growled, the sound echoed off the brick walls of the alley behind the Heavenly Sky Burger outlet where she worked. The one thing about time travel Graham Wafers didn't tell them was the exact time coordinates of arrival didn't necessarily coincide with her strict dietary needs.

She looked wistfully at the chronometer again. She was fifteen minutes off her meal schedule. She patted her ample belly and pressed the button on her belt which would bring her chair to her. She had left the chair for her daily exercise. If you were going to eat six meals a day you had to exercise.

Part 4

It was simple math. And she understood simple. She'd majored in simple at Burger U as part of her degree in Restaurant Domination and Market Saturation (with a minor in employee subjugation).

"Hey! Trix! What's holding ya up out here?"

Trixie turned her ample frame toward the direction of the voice calling to her. She winced again as water in her socks squished between her toes. That'll teach me to get daily exercise.

Who she saw made her wrinkle her brow in annoyance. It wasn't Cherry Bomb calling her, it was that creepy grease stain, Kelp Shaker. She really didn't like Kelp. He played tricks on her.

Like the time....she arched an eyebrow. Hold on. This is six weeks ago.

As she recalled, Kelp was about to play his next trick on her. Two days from now he was going to glue a banana popsicle in the bottom of the spare freezer, the chest freezer. He knew her love for anything banana flavored. (Whoever said the banana burger was a bad idea had a pizza for a brain!)

Two days from now Kelp would tell her the last lonely banana popsicle he'd found was at the bottom of the freezer then, when she peered in and bent over to try and retrieve it, he would shove her in and close the lid.

This timeline's Cherry was on holiday visiting a sick friend on Lollipop III. Unfortunately this meant Trixie's eventual rescuer was a very irate Mr. Pickles-On-The-Side.

Her boss was unimpressed that she had apparently fallen into the freezer and could have died. This HSB outlet had a perfect safety record and he didn't want it jeopardized by her stupidity (at least that's what he told her). She of course couldn't squeal on Kelp because she'd played a few pranks on him too. Since they'd both played the tricks on company time they could both be fired.

They were each other's fat and sassy alibi. Trixie cringed at the thought, but she had no choice. For now.

Note to reader: it was a good thing the Cherry from this time was on holiday. At least they didn't have to explain two orphaned Cherry Bomb's when there was only supposed to be one in the entire galaxy. (What can I say? Time travel creates all sorts of unexpected problems.)

"Hey, Kelp! I'm coming back in right now. Trixie boarded her chair and directed it to entrance at the rear of the HSB outlet. For some reason Kelp held the door open for her until she passed. It closed behind her with a bang.

Part 4

Kelp had a silly grin splitting his pudgy features. This made her suspicious. Kelp hated her as much as she hated him. What was he up to? He had to be up to no good, that much was certain.

"What's goin' on, Kelp?" she said. Her eyes narrowed. "You look way too happy."

"Mr. Pickles-On-The-Side wants to see you in his office right away."

"What about?" She asked. Kelp only shrugged in response.

Trixie had to stop herself from throwing her giant sized cup of soda in his face to wipe that stupid grin off his mug. If she did that she'd be thirsty, and he'd have the satisfaction of knowing he'd gotten to her. Neither was acceptable.

Instead, she offered him a slight smile by curling the corners of her mouth and nodded. Then she directed her chair to carry her to the manager's office at the back of the restaurant.

Mr. Pickles-On-The-Side's office was located at the end of a long, slate gray hallway lit by rows of light bars that ran its length. There were a lot of doors on either side the lengthy corridor.

Many of the rooms behind those doors she'd never even been in even though she'd worked here for over two years.

In fact she didn't even know how many there were exactly, though each time she flew her chair down here there seemed to be more than the last time.

Every time she went to her boss' office she wondered if the nuclear battery in her chair would run out. Silly thought really, but it was a long way to the end of the hall. It took her ten minutes to arrive outside her boss' office.

She grasped the end of the straw, coming from her soda in the chair arm cup holder and put it in her mouth. She took three long swigs of the deliciously sweet grape flavored soda to calm her nerves. (Tuesday was grape day; Wednesday orange, Thursday lemon-lime, Friday's root beer. Saturday was option day when she could choose any flavor she liked. She experimented with some doozys on Saturdays; pineapple, persimmon, grapefruit, and chili-chocolate. She discovered she enjoyed chili-chocolate.)

She didn't know exactly why she was nervous, but she was. This meeting hadn't happened in her six weeks ago. It meant something had created a new timeline.

Part 4

In time travel anything was possible, because any slight deviation, turning right instead of left, or calling in sick because you are a secret agent on a mission to save the future, or you brushed your teeth yourself rather than use an auto-teeth-cleanser, can change the current timeline. When even minor a variance occurred, a new timeline was created. If the deviation was too great the future could be totally disrupted and you might even erase yourself.

The last one was ridiculous. Who brushed their own teeth?

Sometimes I'm too silly even for me.

Then again, as her time travel professor at Burger U, Dr. Paradox, once said, "Time is fluid and it can be flushed down the toilet far too easily."

She reached out and swiped the palm of her right hand over the knocking plate recessed into the doorframe.

"Who goes there?" Mr. Pickles-On-The-Side's gruff voice growled from the speaker set in the wall next to the door.

The speaker was voice activated, of course. "It's Trixie Aioli, sir."

"Come in." The door swooshed as it slid aside so she could enter.

What Trixie saw made her freeze and any moisture in her mouth her mouth dry up. Cherry was already in her bosses office waiting with her boss. And Cherry's eyes were telling her she was in trouble. In fact their whole mission might be in trouble. It was as if the deep fryers pilot light had gone out, and that could signal the end of the world.

***

A slippery slope is best covered with grease, particularly the dirty kind.

— from the speech by General Spear Pickles-and-Cheese (AKA Old Salty Snack) just before his victory at the battle for Lettuce II during the Great Condiments Skirmish of 2453

Trixie swallowed, or rather attempted to, but her mouth was too dry. She considered taking a sip of cola from her soda cup, but Mr. POS (the staff refers to him as POS behind his back) was scowling fiercely and waving her inside. Trixie moved her chair inside his office and the door swooshed shut behind her. She was now officially trapped.

She moved to a position with her chair hovering in front of his large gray plasti-steel desk beside Cherry who stood watching her silently, waiting.

Part 4

The picture of POS with the CEO, his dark eyes smiling seemed to pierce her to her soul.

Cherry being so quiet unnerved her. She wasn't a conversationalist by any means, but this situation was giving her a sour stomach. True Cherry rarely said much of anything unless prompted to do so, or she just felt like it, but couldn't she give some sign of hope?

Mr. POS rested his thin elbows on the arms of his hover chair and steepled his fingers in front of him. His dark beady eyes drifted from Trixie to Cherry then back again.

He cleared his throat then spoke. "So, Aioli and Bomb, I understand you two want a few days off with pay." His eyes narrowed. "Is this true?"

Trixie stole a glance at Cherry who nodded her head ever so slightly to indicate she should take the lead. Trixie knew the truth was Cherry was a very poor liar, being a security specialist and all, so she would have to come up with something. It suddenly occurred to Trixie the direct approach might work best in these circumstances.

"Well, sir, where ever did you get an idea like that?"

Mr. POS chuckled grimly.

"Com'on now, Aioli, let's not play that little game, shall we. Do you and Bomb need a couple of days off or not? It's a simple question."

Trixie shrugged. "If it's not too much trouble, sir, then yes we would."

POS dropped his arms to his sides and eased back in his chair. He arched one eyebrow. Trixie heard Cherry shuffle her feet in the quiet office. "Trouble? Really?" POS snorted. "Of course it's trouble. You both well know finding replacements for your shifts for unscheduled days off is difficult and I'll have to authorized triple pay to cover for you two. Then my salary budget will be over this month, and I'll miss my bonus target. I haven't missed a bonus in twenty seven years."

Mr. POS floated his chair around his desk. As he did Trixie stole a glance at Cherry. She winced. Cherry hadn't told POS anything so who had? Kelp didn't know anything, and if he did she'd just blackmail him like she always did and buy his silence with another hole card. The moron was one slip up away from demotion, or explosion, whichever came first.

Mr. POS stopped at a blank wall. He pressed a button on his chair arm and the wall shimmered. The wall wasn't blank it was a disguised vid monitor.

Part 4

A pang of envy formed in pit of Trixie's belly. She wished she could one day afford such an expensive toy. Not that her own wall vid wasn't good, it's just that it wasn't able to disguise itself. Newer features were always the envy of your friends. Especially on big days like election coverage, or when the new fast food recipes were announced, or when the Food Olympics were on.

After the image steadied there appeared an old man eating from a basket of fries. He was a very old man. "Aioli and Bomb, this is a big man in the world of catering."

Trixie studied the old man munching on his mouthful of fries seemingly oblivious to them watching. Bits of chewed potatoes were falling from the sides of his mouth like rain around the heaping basket. His bulbous cheeks were engorged with food, and his gray hair looked sleek. He wore the usual simple one piece jumpsuit most people did these days.

Trixie shrugged. "Sorry, boss, but I don't get it. He's a handsome fella I'll give ya that, but he doesn't look familiar."

POS sighed. "He had an accident two years ago. A grease fire on Mustard III. He saved three employees, but was badly burned.

A week of surgery to reconstruct his face and injections of fat cells to bring back his rosy cheeks and what you see is the result. He's been laying low for the past two years." POS extended his chest and a wide grin formed on his lips.

Trixie almost ran out of the room when her boss suddenly broke into a grin. POS' split mouth filled with jagged teeth and a trail of drool running out one side and down his cheek was really frightening. His natural state was scowl.

"Uhhh, sir, then who is he?" said Cherry finally saying something. Trixie shifted her gaze to her friend and nodded her approval.

"That, ladies is Cheddar Macaroni." POS crossed his arms as best as he was able over his wide chest, grinning like a kid with his first large burger and fries meal in front of him, and nodded approvingly at the vid screen.

Trixie looked at the screen, but still didn't recognized the old man. He didn't look like any big shot caterer. And she had no idea who Cheddar Macaroni was supposed to be. She'd never heard of him, but her boss seemed to think he was a big deal. She decided to feign interest.

"Wow, Mr. Pickles-On-The-Side, Cheddar Macaroni...impressive."

Part 4

She paused and arched an eyebrow. "How does this have anything to do with us? Sir." She added the last word so he wouldn't get mad at such an impertinent question, but her patience was running as thin as the special sauce used on Taco Planet's Mexi-Dog, and she was tired of waiting for him to get to the point.

POS' grin faded and she was relieved when his familiar scowl returned in all its forehead-wrinkled glory. "You and Bomb will be part of the catering staff for an upcoming event catered by Macaroni Event Planning."

"And why would we do that? We work for HSB not him." Her carefully planned out plot to disrupt Herman Pug's impending marriage of doom to pizza heiress Zippy Piner was fast melting like an ice cream bath on a hot day.

Mr. POS moved his chair back behind his desk and glared at them. "Because, Aioli, he's a major shareholder in HSB, and a personal friend of the CEO. The CEO is my cousin so I naturally volunteered you two." He indicated the picture over his desk with a nod of his head.

"Because we're the best?" asked Cherry, without hesitation.

Good question, thought Trixie.

One corner of POS' mouth curled slightly and his eyes smiled. "No, because you two are my most expendable. At the conclusion of any event cater by Macaroni Catering the last two employees hired are fired. As it happens my cousin is sleeping with the last two girls hired so he doesn't want them fired." His eyes narrowed. "It means you two will be the sacrificial deep fried chicken bombs."

Trixie's heart began to beat rapidly and her hands began to tremble. "But, sir this means if we're fired from them then —"

"Yes, yes, you'll be fired from us as well. So?"

Trixie snorted. "Isn't it obvious? We refuse. You'll have to fire us now."

"OK, you're fired."

Just like that! We're fired!

Cherry took a step closer to POS' desk. Trixie was pleased when POS actually backed his chair away from his desk. "Wait, sir, we'll take the job." Trixie eyes shot to her friend whose mouth was hanging open. Cherry nodded at her indicating with her palms open to hold on.

Trixie couldn't believe her ears. Cherry wanted them to be sucked in to work for someone that would end her lazy spiral to the top of the burger heap.

"Who's the event for, sir?" Cherry asked.

Part 4

Now POS just looked smug. Trixie had to use all her willpower to stop from floating around his desk and strangling the guy. "Why Herman Pug and Zippy Piners wedding, naturally."

Trixie shuddered. In a day full of shocks this was the shock of shocks. They were going to be caterers at the wedding of the man she needed to achieve her career ambitions. Herman had invented the star drive that would ensure the future of the corporation who controlled the technology, and he was marrying someone else. And the event where her career would end before it even started.

Could this day get any worse?

Part 5

A burger is a dish best served medium or medium rare or well done...ya know, however you like it...provided it's cooked that way, or maybe not...oh, whatever!

- Berry McFlipout, Head Chef, Heavenly Sky Burger at a press conference in 2989.

COLD SOAPY WATER LEAKING from the auto washer bot's dishwashing compartment flowed out onto the title floor to splash over Trixie's sneakers. Her socks had barely dried out, now her feet were soaked again. She made a mental note to pack more socks next time she time traveled, and to never to get out of her hover chair ever again in the future.

Or, was it in the past or to the past? Her head hurt, just like it did every time she thought about time travel. I should never have agreed to this ridiculous scheme, she thought. But she knew she had no choice.

Her futures, future depended on the success of this mission.

What annoyed her most was the equipment in the entertainment complex kitchen. it appeared to be as old, as if it'd been used by the ancient Greeks. In fact, when she first entered the kitchen, accompanied by her friend and fellow time traveler, Cherry Bomb, the heavy musk in the air knocked her senses back. She imagined ancient Greece must have smelled a lot like this awful place.

Down the center of the sixty-foot long kitchen was a stainless steel table where the plate set-ups would be done. On one side of the table were rows of walk-in freezers, on the other side were alternating cooking stations, between deep fryers for cooking the fired food delicacies and flattops for grilling frozen burger patties. At least Macaroni served the two most honored foods in the galaxy. No doubt HSB supplied the flash frozen food for the wedding banquet (along with a few credits under the grill for Mr. Pickles-On-The-Side).

Macaroni Event Planning had to be the cheapest catering company in the galaxy. Or maybe it was just old Cheddar Macaroni who was so cheap.

Her boss, Mr. Pickles-On-The-Side hadn't offered them any additional wages to work this wedding as extra employees for Macaroni's operation for Herman Pug's wedding to Zippy Piner.

Now her nose wrinkled under assault of the lilac scented soap blended with the warm water leaking machine. She thought about quitting on the spot and going home, but then she'd run into her other self in this timeline. Cherry reminded her if they quit this job old POS would fire them for sure. If they stayed, then they had a chance, however slim, of saving their jobs. The odds of them keeping their jobs was dropping rapidly.

Trixie sighed then retrieved the controller for the mop-bot which was hung off a hook on the wall. She pressed the on button on the control that unlocked the hidden compartment near the large dehydrator across the cavernous kitchen. It sprung open and the mop-bot rolled out. It hummed softly then glided on it's antigrav cushion across the floor. The bot began to sweep back and forth across the tiled floor with long strands of specially designed water absorbent material sopping up the water.

Part 5

Not that it would do much good. The autowasher wouldn't stop leaking water until the internal tank holding several gallons of water emptied completely.

But there was no use telling any of this to the mop-bot. The bots did their job until it was done even if it took hours or even days.

Trixie's brow wrinkled. She had other potatoes to fry. They had travelled six weeks into the past to stop the impending wedding of her chosen mate and her greatest rival. The stakes were too high and were making her stomach nervous. And a nervous stomach could lead to real trouble, such as not being able to sleep or eat. And not being able to eat could lead to weight loss. And weight loss could lead to no chance of promotion. Skinny people never got promoted. While it was illegal to discriminate against skinnies everyone knew it happened all the time.

Worse of all, if she didn't marry Herman then Zippy would control the new star drive Herman invented. As heir apparent to the Galaxy Pizza empire Zippy would then control the Marketeer Fleet. The star ships would get the new engine thus gaining the edge over Heavenly Sky Burger.

It would mean Trixie's ambition to be CEO of HSB and her plan to raise HSB to the number one spot from number 151 of 152 on Food E-Zine's Annual List of Most Successful Fast Food Chains would end as well.

The only good news today was the impending nuptials scheduled for later today had been delayed until a shipment of genetically modified beef arrived from Home On The Range III. The marketeer ship carrying the valuable cargo had been delayed by few days due to a sudden intrusion of a Big Ball of paper cups into the HOTR system. Trixie had never been so thankful for the Big Ball garbage disposal system. And to think she had once criticized the system for its randomness, and the possible danger to inhabited systems.

If instead she had control of the new drive it would be her ticket to the top of HSB. And then she could finally end the rounding up of the customer's burger checks that kept the company back from the number one spot amongst the fast food companies.

But in the original timeline the wedding wouldn't take place until six months from now.

Part 5

An event, or a sudden change of minds (as ridiculous as it sounded), or something altered in the timeline, had accelerated the wedding date. Trixie turned her head to look at Cherry and saw she was ignoring her. Odd. Why?

"Cherry?" The security specialist turned her head to fix her eyes on her. The aliens red eyes drooped at the corners. Trixie knew what this meant. Cherry was the only survivor of an extinct race wiped out in a war over six hundred years ago by the Cracker King, a despot tyrant from the Late Night Snack System. When Cherry's eyes drooped at the corners it meant she was concealing something. "What's going on?"

"What are you talking about, Trixie?" The security specialist's tone had the gruff edge signaling she was going into her defensive mode. Now Trixie was certain Cheery had hidden an import tidbit of information from her. They knew each other wayyy too well. I really gotta get some new friends.

"OK, my friend, stop cutting the cheese so thick and tell me what's happened. Herman and Zippy's wedding day has been moved up, and you know soemthing about the reasons why that you're not telling me." She crossed her arms over her chest and glared at her partner in time.

Cherry let the air expel from her lungs through her wide nostrils. "OK, ya got me. Graham Wafer told me something important before we came here..." Her words trailed off and the color of her face turned a softer shade more like a red number 3 than her usual red number 40. Her voice dropped to a whisper and her eyes looked down at the floor. "I should have told you earlier, especially when we discovered a few little things had changed. And of course when you decided to fix Kelp by shoving him in that freezer like he planned to do to you in the other timeline." Cherry rolled her eyes. "That really changed things in this new timeline."

Cherry cleared her throat then continued. "Truth is our being in the here and now disrupted the time stream. The future has been shattered. I have no idea what's going to happen."

Trixie swallowed hard and her stomach growled. The situation had just gone from crappy to we're-doomed-to-die-foodless. She had to think of a solution fast.

***

Pizza is one thing, burgers are another.
- Sippy Fluffy, 403 President of The United Dirt Republic speaking at his inaugural speech in 3000. The speech was controversial because it mentioned pizza before burgers, something no president had ever done. President Fluffy was assassinated in 3002 and a 1/32nd

Part 5

Trixie pounded on Graham Wafers front door rather than pressing the com button. Her breathing was rapid and her heart pounded hard in her chest. She pressed one corner of her hover chair repeatedly against the door of the man who ruined her life. The plasti-steel door bent inward under the force of each blow then bounced back to it's original shape. She had considered using the com unit affixed to a steel pole next to the front steps, but dismissed the idea in favor of direct assault against Wafers house. The use of force was sanctioned by the seemingly insurmountable predicament his actions had placed her in.

The com unit, dented and the peeling red paint, was old fashioned, but not surprising in this neighborhood. Wafers resided in the original section of Fast Food City near the site of the first fast food restaurant of the franchise wars, Flamer Burger & Pizza & Donuts & Fried Chicken. After Galaxy Pizza and Heavenly Sky Burger came into being, with their niche marketing specializing in each food group of fast food, the multi-market chains like FBPDFC were crushed under the wheels of progress like an old fashioned soda cup. They went from serving millions of meals a week to zero in a few short months.

Naturally, these outlets employed whole neighborhoods, such as this one, so thousands of people were thrown out of work. That coupled with the rise of labor saving bots replacing more jobs for humanoids drove the area into poverty pretty quickly. Her nose wrinkled under the assault of the odor coming from the Pont l'Eveque — the galaxy's stinkiest cheese — factory in the area.

Of course, the local conditions made Trixie wonder why Graham Wafers lived in such a neighborhood. He'd certainly charged them enough to make the time trip, and he didn't even have a frequent traveler program. Surely he had sufficient funds to blow this dump and move to a condo or apartment on the good side of town, maybe even next to an HSB outlet. Those units were the most coveted in the real estate market

She had the urge to kick herself for not asking him about this before they time traveled. The key to his poverty had to be the key to her getting back to her own time and repairing this nightmare she'd been sucked into.

Trixie glanced over her shoulder at Cherry, who was pacing back and forth on the sidewalk at the end of the cracked walkway.

Part 5

Cherry had her hands behind her back pacing, but stopping occasionally to focus her attention on the front door of Graham Wafer's house. Trixie could sense her friends nervous energy even these few yards apart.

She caught the four-limbed, two-headed, four-eyed alien's attention by waving for her to join her on the front step. Cherry shook her head, then looked away returning once again to her pacing the sidewalk. Trixie frowned then turned back to thumping her chair into the front door. What had gotten into her friend? Was she scared of something? Or was she upset about not telling her everything Graham had warned her about the risks with time travel. Then again would she have listened? Probably not. She desperately wanted to stop the wedding. She would have accepted any risks to accomplish that objective.

The door suddenly swung inward not all the way just partially. Odd. The door must have been unlocked. Trixie scowled at the door. No one in this neighborhood would leave a door unlocked. Not even a fool like Wafers.

She scolded herself for being so quick to judge. She didn't know if he was a fool, an idiot, or a genius for that matter. She knew nothing about Graham Wafers, other than she knew Cherry and he were friends.

She concluded her frustration with their situation must be beginning to show. Past experience told her failure to control her emotions often led to losing her head at a critical moment, and that would be so not good.

"Cherry!" she called to her friend. Cherry appeared at her side just as she nudged the door with a corner of her hover chair causing it to swing open wide enough so they could see a figure laying on it's back on the carpeted floor five or six feet from the now open door. Trixie had to squeeze her nostrils between her fingers when the smell of stale hot fudge nearly overwhelmed her.

She floated her chair tentatively (yes, hover chairs can float tentatively) inside Wafers house until she saw, what she thought at first was a shadow over his plump body was in fact hot fudge. It clung to his body like a glove which as why it had fooled her at first.

Cherry stepped inside behind her. The security specialist whistled softly through on of her three nostrils. "Wow. How did that happen?"

Trixie glanced at Cherry. "Can't you smell it?"

"What?" She moved closer to Wafers and her eyes narrowed as she studied the substance he lay in.

"Oh, Chocolate. Hot fudge to be precise. My race can't smell chocolate or derivatives of chocolate."

Trixie nodded. Her heart ached for her friend. An inability to smell chocolate must be a horrible disability.

She moved her chair closer to Wafers. He's dead alright. His chest wasn't rising and falling. Pressing the com button on her chair arm the vocal command bot activated. "Number please," said the bot's female voice. Ever since her parents bought her the Diamond Elite hover chair as a present for Franchise Founders Day she'd wanted to change the com unit's voice interface, but had never found the time. She especially didn't like the bots attitude parameters.

"Get me police HQ."

"The cops?" said the bot. "Cool."

"Never mind the editorial comments. Just connect me."

"OK, OK. Hold onto your knickers." A small blue light next to the unit on the chair came on.

Trixie had no idea what a knicker was exactly even though it did sounded vaguely like the name of a snack food. "Police," a deep male voice said over the com unit speaker.

She cleared her throat and replied. "Yes, hello. This is Trixie Aioli. I'm at Graham Wafers house and — "

"Did you say Graham Wafers?" interrupted the police officer.

Trixie's eyes flitted to Cherry who mouthed she better hang up. "I've a bad feeling about this," she added in a whisper. Trixie held up a hand to silence her friend. This is the police what's the worse that can happen?

"Yes, officer, Graham Wafer."

"Well, we've been looking for him for a long time." She heard a click. "We've locked onto to your com signal unit in your hover chair. A unit will be there in seven point two minutes. Do not leave. We will question you. Mega Fried Banana Branch out." The connection light blinked out, but began to flash intermittently.

Trixie's stomach muscles tightened. "Com unit," she began between gritted teeth, "who did you call?"

"Uhhh...the MFBB of course."

"I told you to call the cops."

The com unit bot chuckled. "No. No. You're in the house of a known fugitive.

Part 5

I'm required to connect to the level of law enforcement consummate with the criminals level of crime. It's the law, ya know." The edge of sarcasm in bot's tone sent a flash of anger through Trixie.

"I think we better get outta here," suggested Cherry. "MFBB interrogations are known to be nasty. I heard once they dip you in stale deep fryer oil until you talk."

Trixie waved one hand over the blue light. "What about this?" The light kept blinking repeatedly; in fact it was blinking faster with each passing second. They MFBB was getting closer. They'd be here soon. If they were arrested they'd never make it back in time to work the wedding. Then they'd be fired and all would be lost.

Cherry scanned the room then rushed to a table where a steel cup sat. She picked it up then moved to Trixie's chair raised it shoulder high then brought it down hard on the com unit's cover. There was a loud cracking sound and the light went out. Cherry threw the cup to the floor then with two of her four hands wrenched off the cover. It landed on the floor next to the cup.

Next she reached in the hole where the cover had been, to yank out the micro circuit board which she also threw to the floor then mashed under the heel of her left shoe.

"Where we gonna go?" she asked Cherry.

"My place."

Trixie knew Cherry lived in the servant district a tough neighborhood if there ever was one. Trash bots maintenance crews, repair techs of every class lived in this corrupt seething mass of human flotsam where life was cheap and being poor made a guy or gal as mean as the streets themselves. At least that's what the vids made about that part of the planet would have you believe.

Cherry told her other stories about the neighborhood of laughing children scampering about on their hover carts playing in the parks and floating in the orbit simulators. She said the movies exaggerated every tiny negative detail about her neighborhood. Sure there were plenty of displaced aliens like herself, but that was to be expected when the jobs they often qualified for, were behind the scenes of the fast food conglomerates.

"Sounds good." Her thoughts were interrupted by the scream of a siren outside on the street. The MFBB had arrived. Time to go.

Part 5

They slipped out the back of Wafers house and made it to one of the automated skyliner stations without being noticed. Soon they boarded the skyliner bound for the servant district. They were whisking across the city with it's magnificent of red, green, yellow, and blue neon and plasti-steel logos signs. The sky was pierced by gleaming corporate towers, bright and shiny from the sunlight bouncing off the hundred floor glass towers and pyramids jutting into the clear blue sky to the horizon. Gazing over the city spread before her like a carpet of diamonds and colorful jewels Trixie vowed one day she'd have an office in one of those magnificent towers.

"So, Cherry, tell me more about the neighborhood where you live. Can we go to a park, is there an HSB outlet near your place?" Trixie felt a twinge of hunger beginning in her stomach. She needed to eat soon. A burger and fries would go down nicely right about now.

"Well..." began Cherry her voice hesitant. Trixie turned her attention to her friend seated across the aisle from her. She was floating in her chair in the empty slots reserved for hover chairs on the other side of the compartment her chair held in pace by antigravity clamps. Cherry's eyes drooped at the corners.

Now what? More bad news? Will this day never end?

"What I told you about my neighborhood wasn't exactly accurate."

Trixie arched an eyebrow. "Oh, yeah, how so?"

"Ummm...you know how I said it wasn't as bad as the vids showed?" Trixie nodded. "It's actually worse than the vids show. Much worse. But the good news is the police and the MFBB are too afraid to enter so at least we'll be safe from them."

Trixie was almost afraid to ask. "And what's the bad news?"

Cherry turned her attention to staring out the window. "My neighbors might kill us."

Trixie realized she better stop saying how bad can it be because this situation had gone from bad to worse to down right fatal. Oh, crap....

To be continued in *Round Up At the Burger Bar Part 6* watch for it to continue the adventures of Trixie Aioli as she strives, slides, and schemes her way to CEO of a large fast food franchise to take over the entire galaxy!

Other titles from 53rd Street Publishing you may enjoy
http://www.53rdstreetpublising.com
Titles as R.G. Crossley

Short Stories

Razor and Edge Mysteries
The Kidnapping of Billy Buttons
String of Pearls
Death by Clown
Beggin' For Murder
Ragged Ice
The Grand Central Mystery
A Strange Case of Undead Murder

Jazz Stiletto Mysteries
A Day Without Sunshine
Skullduggery
Instrument of Justice

Non-Series Mysteries
Mirror Image
Dangerous Waters
Cape Disappointment
Boomerang
The Watcher of Wayburn Street
The Apprentice
Drip!
A Beautiful Friendship and The Parrot of Doom
Robine's Diary
The Christmas Club
Loose Ends

Splatter Pattern
It Takes Two

Anthologies
The Adventures of Razor and Edge:
Five Tales From The Quirky Detective Team

Novels
A Bad Case of Loyalty
The Last Serial Killer
Shear Murder

Titles as Russ Crossley

Novels
Attack of the Lushites
Revenge of the Lushites

Short Stories
Countdown
Shoeless Moe
Round Up At The Burger Bar:
The Story of Trixie Pug, Parts 1, 2, 3, 4, 5, 6, 7
Five Minutes
Blossom Queen, Barbarian
The Secret
The Family Line
End of the Flies
Death by Magic
The Penguin Sleeps With The Fishes
Only The Worthy
Hero For A Day

End of Empire
Strange Bedfellows
Big Business
A Perfect Crime
The Wise Guy and The Pirates
In Search of the Perfect Cup
T.I.N. Men
The Legend of G and the Dragonettes
The Incredible Mr. Fix-It
Lock Stock and Barrel
Divided Loyalties
Cave of Wonders
A Family Empire
Until We Meet Again
Dragon Rising

Presents Anthology Series
Tales of Urban Fantasy
Five Tales of Bizarre Detectives
Tales of Mystery and Suspense
Tales of Weird Fantasy
Spies, Detectives, & Heroes
Tales of Twisted Crime
Tales of The Unexpected
Tales From Space
10 by Russ Crossley
Round Up At The Burger Bar: The Story of Trixie Pug,
Parts 1- 5 The Beginning
Worlds of Science Fiction and Fantasy
More Tales of Mystery and Suspense
Ladies of the Jolly Roger
Justice Served

Titles as R.G. Hart

Short Stories
Tikka's Big Day
"My Partner the Zombie" —
Hungry For Your Love Anthology
(St. Martin's Press)
Big Hairy Deal
One Red Shoe
A Bad Day in Lunden Texas
Hook Island
Grind Manor
Bloody Betty, Queen of the Pirates

Anthologies
Love Stories
Ladies of the Jolly Roger with R.S. Meger

Novels
My Zombie Prince
Antique Virgin
The Fire In Their Hearts
with R.S. Meger from Champagne Books
Zomopolis

Non-Fiction
The Writers Tools - The Synopsis

Also available from 53rd Street Publishing

In the year 4444 and a 1/4 the Lushites have returned. Piper Cleaner, First Assistant to the Assistant Surveillance Officer discovers a Lushite intergalactic vessel heading their way.

Alarm bells ring throughout the galaxy! Have the Lushites returned to seek revenge?

Join Piper and Major Virginia Slim on a crazy, outrageous ride across the galaxy in the far future where addictions are rampant and conspiracies thrive.

The second book in War of the Lushites series is a satirical space opera revealing the future of addiction.

Available in an electronic edition for at your favorite online retailer.

It is also available in trade paperback from various book retailers. Order it at a bookstore near you.

(